CHIK CHAK SHABBAT

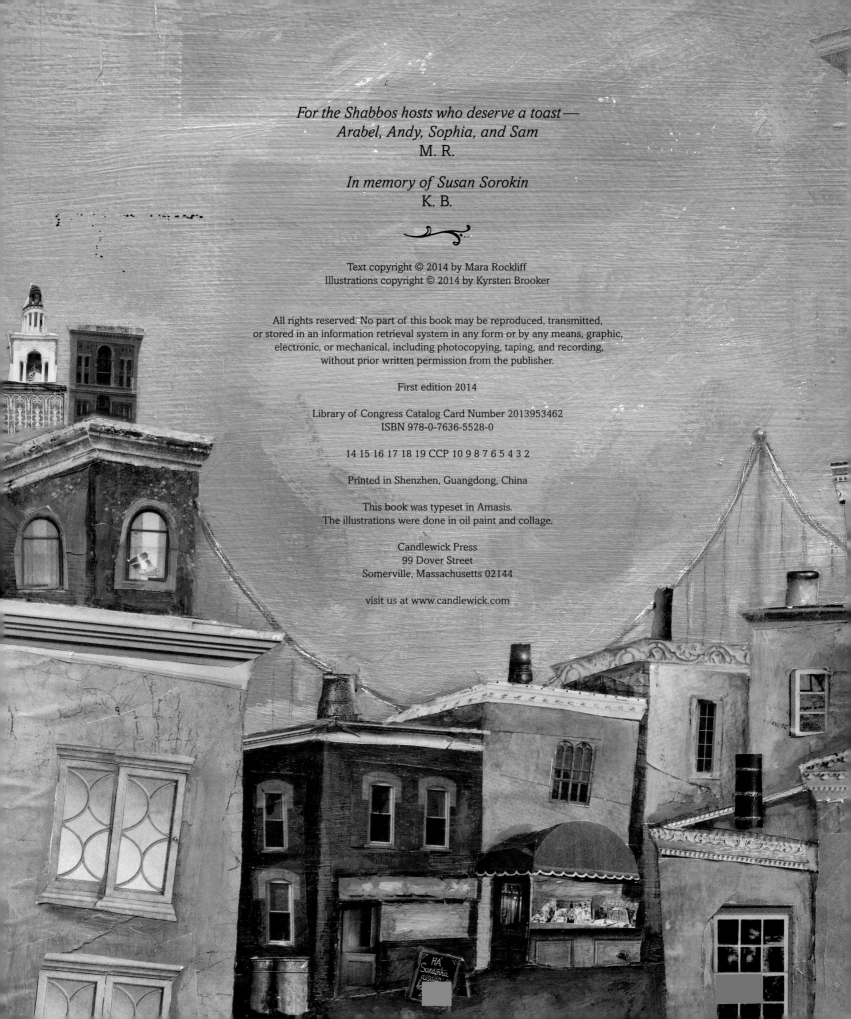

For the Shabbos hosts who deserve a toast—
Arabel, Andy, Sophia, and Sam
M. R.

In memory of Susan Sorokin
K. B.

First edition 2014

Library of Congress Catalog Card Number 2013953462
ISBN 978-0-7636-5528-0

14 15 16 17 18 19 CCP 10 9 8 7 6 5 4 3 2

Printed in Shenzhen, Guangdong, China

This book was typeset in Amasis.
The illustrations were done in oil paint and collage.

Candlewick Press
99 Dover Street
Somerville, Massachusetts 02144

visit us at www.candlewick.com

CHIK CHAK SHABBAT

Mara Rockliff   illustrated by Kyrsten Brooker

CANDLEWICK PRESS

Every Saturday, a wonderful smell wafted from apartment 5-A.

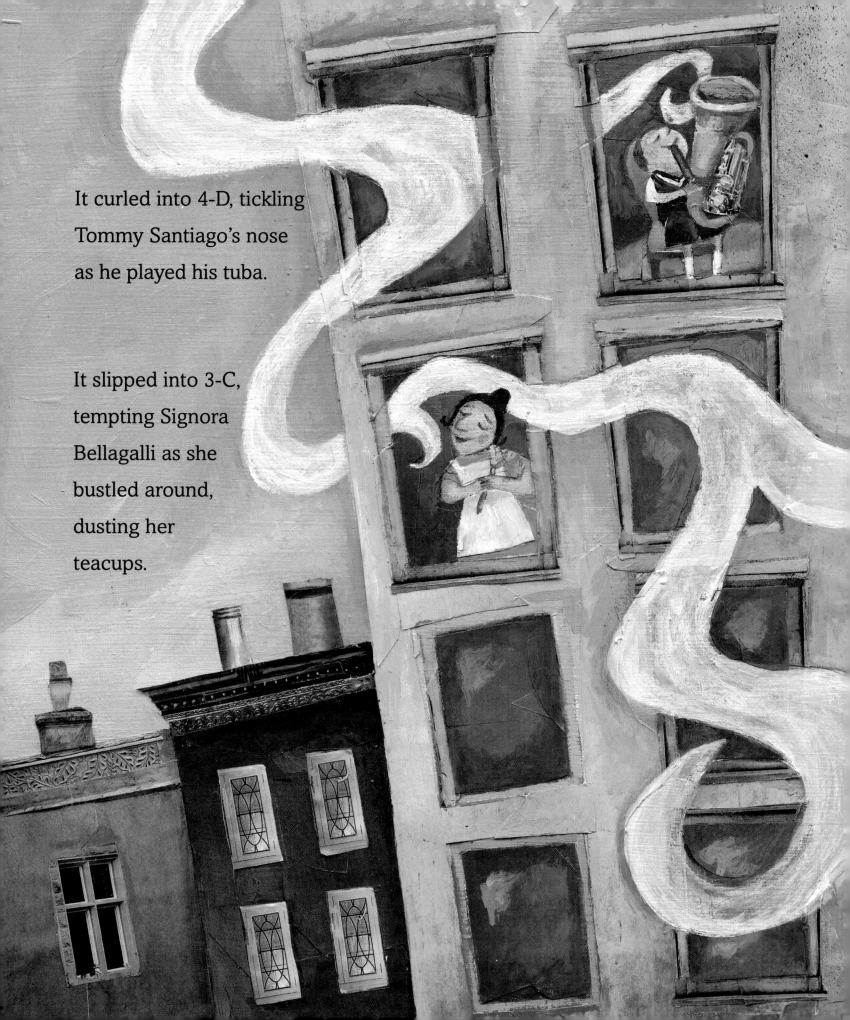

It curled into 4-D, tickling Tommy Santiago's nose as he played his tuba.

It slipped into 3-C, tempting Signora Bellagalli as she bustled around, dusting her teacups.

It crept under the door
of 2-B, tantalizing
Mr. Moon as he sat
typing his new
romance novel.

Even the Omar family
on the first floor caught
a whiff. They sniffed
the air and smiled.

At last, the door to 5-A flew open. Out stepped Goldie Simcha, her face shining like a silver spoon.

"Come in! Come in!
It's *cholent* time!"

As her neighbors took their places at her table,
Goldie ladled steaming stew into their bowls.

While they ate, they argued about what made
Goldie's *cholent* so delicious.

Signora Bellagalli cried,
"It's the tomatoes!"

"Or the barley?"
offered Mr. Moon.

Little Lali Omar piped up,
"The potatoes!"

And the Santiagos all agreed
it had to be the beans.

But Goldie shook her head.

"When I was a girl," she said, "I always helped my grandmother
get ready for Shabbat. All Friday afternoon, we rushed around:

cutting up vegetables,

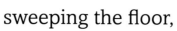

sweeping the floor,

dressing the table in its
best lace tablecloth.

Busy-busy, hurry-hurry, do it right away, *chik chak*!

But when the sun went down, my grandma lit the candles and Shabbat began."

"For one whole night and day, we put aside the things
that kept us busy all week long.

While the *cholent* bubbled slowly on the stove, we spent
time in a special way—together."

"I don't celebrate Shabbat exactly as my grandma did," said Goldie. "But every Friday afternoon, I put a pot of *cholent* on the stove to bubble through the night and day. And when it's done at last, it has a special taste that isn't beans or barley, or tomatoes or potatoes. For me, the taste of *cholent* is . . . Shabbat."

And all her neighbors raised their spoons and said, "Shabbat!"

One Saturday, however, something wasn't right.

Tommy's tuba played nothing but sour notes.

Signora Bellagalli's nicest teacup tumbled off the shelf and smashed.

And Mr. Moon, exasperated, hurled the pages of his latest romance novel right across the room.

The Omars sniffed and sniffed but couldn't catch the faintest whiff.

At last, little Lali Omar climbed the stairs and knocked on Goldie's door.

Goldie answered, her face buried in a tissue. "Friday afternoon, I felt too sick to get the *cholent* on the stove," she said, and sniffled. "Now it's too late. You can't make *cholent* in a hurry, right away, *chik chak*!"

No *cholent* for Shabbat!

Tommy Santiago dropped his tuba
when he heard the news.

Signora Bellagalli's feather
duster flew into the air.

Mr. Moon got so mixed up,
he put a monster robot in his
romance novel and it squashed
the hero flat.

On the first floor, the Omars frowned.

"Poor Goldie," Mrs. Omar said.

"It just won't be Shabbat for her," Mr. Omar agreed.

Little Lali peered into the fridge. "Potato curry isn't the same thing as *cholent,*" she said. "Still, it always cheers me up."

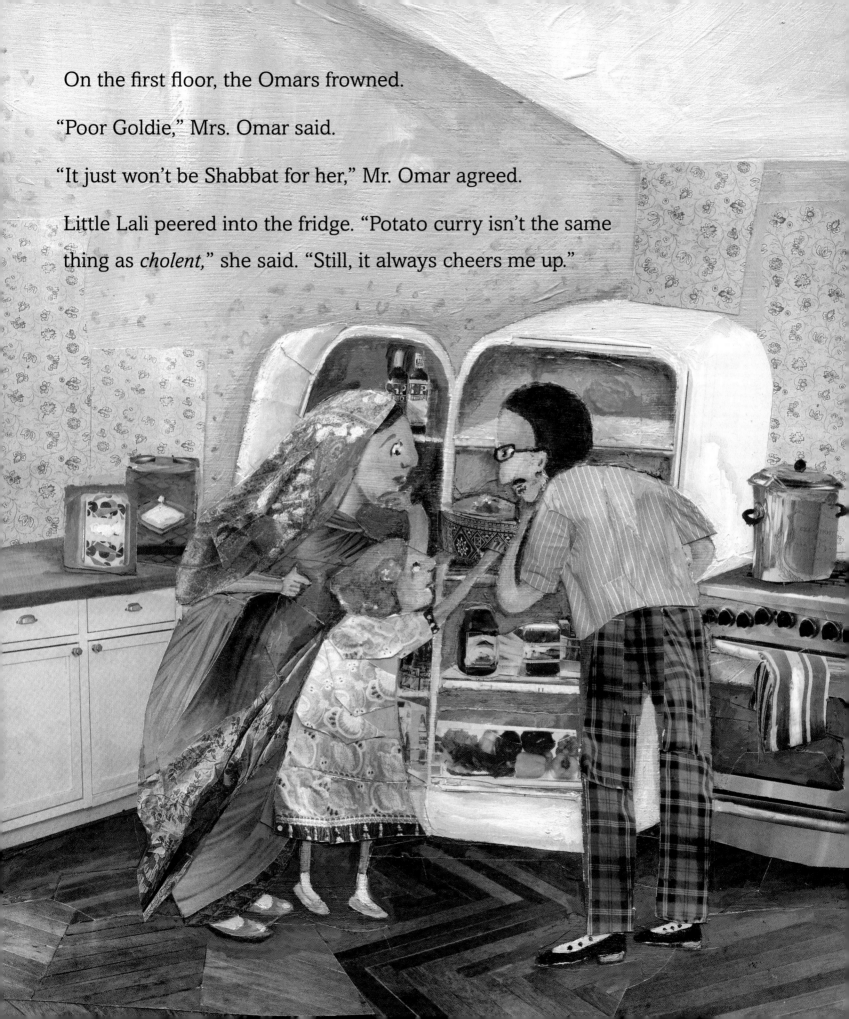

As the Omars climbed the stairs with their bowl of potato curry,
Mr. Moon came out of 2-B with a tray.

"Korean barley tea," he told them.

"Of course, it isn't *cholent*, but . . ."

Signora Bellagalli squeezed out of 3-C.

"Tomato pizza," she puffed. "It's not *cholent,* but . . ."

Tommy Santiago held the door of 4-D open for his mother.

"It's not *cholent,*" she admitted cheerfully. "But everyone likes beans and rice."

Goldie opened the door for them. She blew her nose, wiped her eyes, and smiled. "Come in! Come in!"

Her neighbors took their places at her table, and they filled their plates.

"We didn't have time to make anything special," Signora Bellagalli apologized. "We had to hurry-hurry, bring it right away, *chik chak*! But . . ."

"But here we are," said little Lali Omar.
"Together."

Goldie took a bite of pizza. A nibble of curry. A mouthful of beans and rice. She sipped her barley tea.

Then she looked around the table, her face shining like a silver spoon, and said, "I think it tastes exactly like Shabbat."

CHOLENT

Goldie's grandmother cooked cholent *with a special cut of meat called flanken, but Goldie's recipe is vegetarian. Either way is good. Just be sure to leave plenty of time, because there is one way you can't cook* cholent: *in a hurry, right away,* chik chak*!*

INGREDIENTS

Olive oil

2 large onions, chopped

28-ounce can diced tomatoes

1 cup barley

4 or 5 potatoes, peeled and cut into chunks

1½ cups dried beans (any kind—Goldie likes to mix garbanzo, white, and pinto beans)

2 carrots, peeled and cut into chunks

Water or vegetable broth

Salt and pepper

DIRECTIONS

1. Heat a big pot on the stove, then pour a little oil in it.

2. When the oil is hot, add the onions and stir until they're fried.

3. Add the tomatoes, barley, potatoes, beans, and carrots.

4. Add enough water or broth to make it stew.

5. Add salt, pepper, and any other flavorings you like.*

6. Bring the stew to a boil, then turn the heat down very low so it simmers.

7. Cook for a long time. All day is good. All night is even better.

8. *B'tayavon!* Eat and enjoy!

*Goldie throws in a couple of bay leaves, a few good squirts of ketchup, and a lot of smoked paprika. You could also try garlic powder, cumin, onion soup mix, or even veggie sausages.

Another fun thing to do is (gently) drop in whole eggs in their shells and let them cook. When the *cholent* is ready, remove the eggs with a slotted spoon and let them cool. Then peel the shells and you'll have *cholent*-flavored hard-boiled eggs!